WEEKLY READER
CHILDREN'S BOOK CLUB
Presents Two Books in One

LITTLE
PEEWEE

Or, Now Open the Box

By DOROTHY KUNHARDT

SYLVESTER

*The Mouse
with the Musical Ear*

By ADELAIDE HOLL

GOLDEN PRESS · NEW YORK

D1238933

Little *Peewee*

OR, NOW OPEN THE BOX

By Dorothy Kunhardt

Illustrated by J. P. Miller

Weekly Reader Book Club Edition

Once there was a circus man with a quite
tall red hat on his head. He had a circus
of his very own, so that was why he was called
the circus man. It was a wonderful, wonderful
circus.

The circus man kept his wonderful circus inside a big red tent.

Every day the circus man stood in front of
his big red tent. He held up something
in his hand, very high for everybody to see.
He held up a teeny, weeny little box.
And he shouted very loud, "Come on, everybody!
Come on over here to my tent. Come on,
everybody. I have something exciting to show you.
Just wait till I show you what I have in this
little box! So hurry up, everybody."

Everybody came running and skipping
and hopping as fast as they could to the circus
man's big red tent.

8

And when everybody was there, the circus man said, "Everybody look now. Everybody look now. Everybody LOOK now. Everybody LOOK!"

Then he opened the box, and out came the
teeniest, weeniest, teeny, teeny, teeny,
weeny, weeny, weeny little dog in all the world.
He was dear little Peewee, the circus dog.

He just stepped out of his teeny, weeny box,
and he looked around at everybody. The minute
he looked around at everybody, everybody loved him.

12

Then the circus man said, "Well, I knew everybody would love my little Peewee. It's too bad
he doesn't know any tricks—not a single one.
Not even how to roll over, not even how to
shake hands. But, never mind. He is so teeny,
weeny that everybody loves him. And that was true.
EVERYBODY loved little Peewee.

There was the clown with two heads, but one
of them was probably make-believe.
He loved little Peewee.

There was the small man who could juggle three ducks all at the same time.

He loved little Peewee.

There was the man sitting on a chair, on top of six tables just going to fall down, and blowing soap bubbles.

He loved little Peewee.

16

There was the lady standing on her head on an
umbrella. With one foot she was holding a pair
of scissors, and with the other foot she was
holding a cup full of nice, warm milk.

She loved little Peewee.

There was the elephant crawling under another
elephant.

He loved little Peewee.

There was the thin man. He loved little Peewee.

There was the strong baby holding up an
automobile with a seal in the back seat.

He loved little Peewee.

There was the snake that could put his tail
in his mouth and then go rolling right up the stairs.

He loved little Peewee.

There was the lady hanging in the air, just by
her nose being tied to a good strong rope.

She loved little Peewee.

There was the fat lady.

She loved little Peewee.

There was the polar bear who could jump up
in the air and click his ice skates together
four times.

He loved little Peewee.

There was the goat that could stand right on a
bed, with the bed all burning up, and not even mind
about the fire being hot.

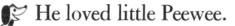 He loved little Peewee.

There was the huge tall giant.
He loved little Peewee.

But one day, a terrible,
frightful, awful thing happened.
One day little Peewee started to grow.

And he grew

and he grew

and he grew

and he grew

until poor little Peewee, the circus dog,
was just the same size as any other plain dog
that you would see anywhere.

Then the circus man cried and said, "Now,
I can't keep you in my circus any more,
dear little Peewee. I am so sorry. If only
you could do some tricks, it would be different.
But you can't do any tricks—not even roll over,
not even shake hands. Now you are just as big
as any plain dog, and how can I keep just a
plain dog in my circus? NO, I just can't, so
we must say goodbye, dear little Peewee."

Then all the whole wonderful circus cried,
and the whole circus said, "Goodbye, dear little
Peewee."

So poor little Peewee started to go away
and never come back to the circus any more.
And JUST THEN, a wonderful, splendid,
beautiful thing happened. As dear little Peewee
was beginning to walk away sadly and slowly . . .
he started to grow again!

and he grew

and he grew

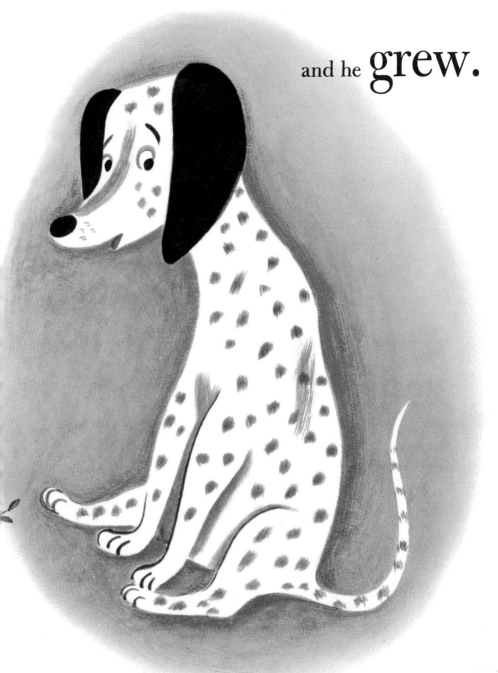

and he **grew.**

Then the circus man said, "Oh, my dearest
little Peewee, now you won't have to go after all.
Now you are so lovely and big, you are the very dog
for my circus!"

So little Peewee stayed in the circus man's
wonderful circus, and everybody loved him.

Every day, just before the circus started,
the circus man would stand outside the big red tent.
Right beside him he would have a huge, enormous box.

Then the circus man would shout,
"Come on, everybody!
Come on over here to my tent! Hurry up, everybody!
I have something exciting to show you! Just wait
till you see what I have in this great, enormous
box! So, hurry up, everybody!"

And everybody would come running and skipping
and hopping to the circus man's wonderful circus
tent. Then the circus man would say, "Come on
inside the tent, everybody, and I will open the
box for you."

Everybody would help the circus man push
and push the great, enormous box into the tent.
Then the circus man would open the top of the great,
enormous box, and out would POP

dear little Peewee. The circus man would say,
"People, this is my dear little circus dog,
Peewee. He is the hugest, most enormous dog in
the whole world, and I love him dearly!"

And every time the circus man said, "He is the
hugest, most enormous dog in the whole world,
and I love him dearly," little Peewee felt

VERY
HAPPY
INDEED!

35

Sylvester

THE MOUSE WITH THE
MUSICAL EAR

By Adelaide Holl
Illustrated by N. M. Bodecker

Sylvester was a country mouse.
He lived in a grassy meadow,
and there were lovely sounds
all about him.

On the north there was a little road
where birds fluttered in the dust
and made little chirping sounds.

On the south there was a lovely woods
where the meadow larks sang, and sang.

On the east there was a cornfield
where soft winds made music all day,
and crickets chirp, chirped all night.

And on the west there was a silver brook
that went gurgle, glub, glub!
with a musical beat.

Sylvester was a mouse
with a musical ear.
He loved the meadow sounds by day.

He loved the meadow sounds by night.
He would sit in his doorway,
listening to the birds and to the crickets.
He would sit, listening
to the winds and to the brook.
He would sit, quiet,
humming softly to himself.

41

But one day men came from the city.
They dug up the little road on the north
and made a big highway.
Now, birds no longer fluttered in the dust
and made little chirping sounds.
Cars went by ZOOM!
Trucks went by WHOOSH!
Sylvester no longer heard
the music of the birds.

Soon down the big highway
the city began to come closer.
One day men came and cut down
the lovely woods on the south.
They put up rows and rows of houses.
Now the meadow larks
no longer sang in the woods.
The meadow larks went away
to sing and sing in another place.

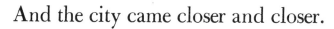

And the city came closer and closer.
Men came once more.
They cut down the cornfield on the east
and put up rows and rows of shops.
The crickets went away
to chirp, chirp in another cornfield.
And Sylvester no longer heard the winds
above the city noises.

The city came closer and closer.

Men came again.

They dug up the silver brook on the west.

Now, it no longer went gurgle, glub, glub!

with a musical beat.

And Sylvester no longer sat in his doorway

humming softly to himself.

He just sat,

listening to the ZOOM! of the cars

and the WHOOSH! of the trucks.

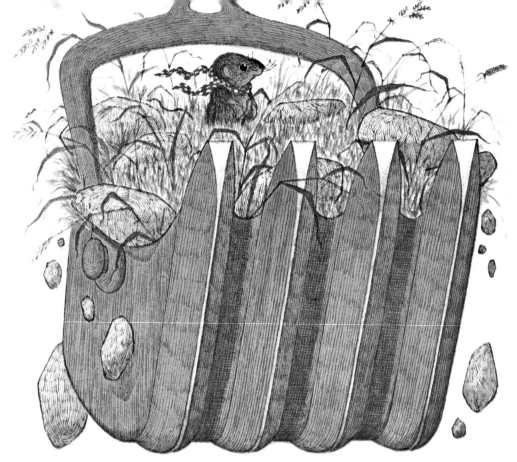

One day men came with a big bulldozer.
They dug up the grassy meadow.
They dug up Sylvester's house.
They even dug up Sylvester.
"I am no longer a country mouse.
I am a city mouse," he said.
"I shall find another home."
And away he went.

There were many places in the city.
But no place was just right
for a mouse with a musical ear.
Some places were too noisy.
And some places were too quiet.
Sylvester went on and on.

All at once he heard lovely sounds.
He heard lovely music. In he went.
And there was a place
filled with musical sounds.
There was a place just right
for a mouse with a musical ear.

Sylvester saw a fine house.
There was a little door
for going in, and for coming out.
Across the doorway was a wire fence.
In went Sylvester, and he sat, quiet,
humming softly to himself.

Sylvester liked his house.
He especially liked the gay music—
piano music, violin music,
and drums with a musical beat.
Sylvester liked his doorway.
He especially liked going in,
and coming out.
When he went across the wire fence,
he made lovely sounds. Plink! Plink!
He made music.

Sylvester was very quiet by day.
But at night, when the shop was dark,
he played on the wire fence
across his doorway.
He played quiet music. Plink! Plink!
He played noisy music. Plonk! Plonk!
He played the music he heard all day.

People went by the shop at night.
"Who is playing?" they asked.
"Who plays music in your shop at night?"
they asked the shopkeeper.

One night the shopkeeper
listened in the dark.
He was very quiet.
Sylvester came softly to his door.

He began to play. Plunk! Plunk! Plunk!
The shopkeeper heard the music.
It came from the guitar on the shelf.
But in the dark he did not see Sylvester.
"It is a magic guitar!" he cried.
"A magic guitar that plays by itself!"

Soon people heard
about the magic guitar.
They stood outside the shop at night
and listened.

54

They went inside the shop by day
and looked.
But nobody would buy the guitar.
Nobody would buy a magic guitar
that played by itself.

Far away in the West, Tex heard
about the magic guitar.
Tex loved music. Tex loved to sing.
But Tex did not have a guitar.
"A guitar is just what I need," said Tex.
"Especially a magic guitar
that plays by itself!"

Away to the city went Tex.

He traveled a long, long way.

He traveled along, singing as he went.

Finally he came to the city.
"Where can I find the magic guitar?"
he asked.
Tex found the magic guitar.
He bought the magic guitar.
Tex was very happy.

Tex set off for the West
with his magic guitar.
He traveled along, singing as he went.
Inside the guitar was Sylvester
sound asleep.
Tex stopped at night to rest
in a grassy meadow.
It was very dark and very quiet.
All at once Tex heard music.
Plink! Plink! Plunk! Plunk! Plonk! Plonk!

Tex sat up, and there was Sylvester!
"It is not a magic GUITAR!" cried Tex.
"It is a magic MOUSE!
A mouse with a musical ear!"
Sylvester stopped playing.
He saw the lovely grassy meadow.
He heard the lovely country sounds.
He looked and looked at Tex.
At once, he and Tex liked one another.
They became great friends.

Sylvester went home with Tex.
He played the guitar while Tex sang.
They made lovely music together.
People came from far away to listen.
They traveled here,
and they traveled there.
They made soft music and noisy music.

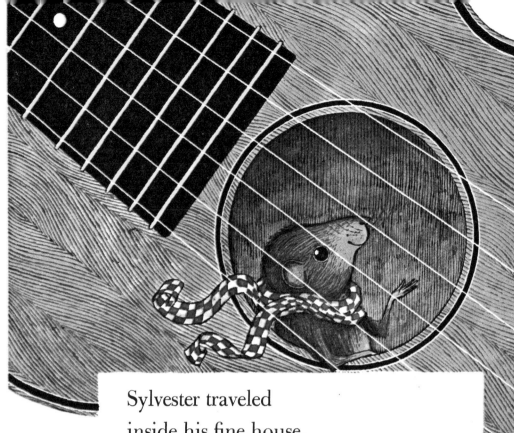

Sylvester traveled
inside his fine house.
And sometimes at night
he would sit, quiet, in his doorway,
humming softly to himself.
Sometimes he was a city mouse,
and sometimes he was a country mouse.
But, at all times,
he was a musical mouse—
a mouse with a musical ear!